The
Ears of
Corn

THE EARS OF CORN

An Ike and Mem Story

BY Patrick Jennings

ILLUSTRATED BY
Anna Alter

HOLIDAY HOUSE / NEW YORK

Library of Congress Cataloging-in-Publication Data
Jennings, Patrick.
The ears of corn/by Patrick Jennings;
illustrated by Anna Alter.—1st ed.
p. cm.—(An Ike and Mem book; 5)
Summary: When Ike and his little sister, Mem, spend the weekend
at their grandparents' farm, they resent all the work they must do,
until they realize that there is more to their visit than just doing chores.
ISBN 0-8234-1770-0 (hardcover)
[1. Farm life—Fiction. 2. Grandparents—Fiction. 3. Work—Fiction.
4. Brothers and sisters—Fiction.] I. Alter, Anna, ill. II. Title.

PZ7.J4298715 Ear 2003
[Fic]—dc21   2001024487

In memory of

Dale and Ina Heiny

—P. J.

THE
EARS OF
CORN

It was Friday night. Ike and his little sister, Mem, were sitting in the backseat, playing I Spy.

"Is it the knob on the radio?" Ike asked.

"Nope," Mem said, smiling.

"Is it Dad's key ring?" Ike asked.

"Nope," Mem said again.

"Then I give up," Ike said.

"It's Mommy's belly button!" Mem said.

"You can't spy Mom's belly button," Ike said. "She's in the front seat."

"I remember what it looks like," Mem said.

The car turned onto a gravel road. Its tires made crunching sounds.

"We're here!" Mem said.

Ike looked out his window and saw his grandparents' huge cornfield. Out Mem's window he saw their old oak trees. Through the trees he could see their farmhouse.

Ike liked visiting the farm. He liked playing in the cornfield and riding the ponies. Sometimes, though, his grandparents invited him and Mem to stay the weekend. Then they had to do a lot of chores. Ike didn't like doing a lot of chores.

"Yeah," Ike said. "We're here."

Grandmother and Grandfather smiled as they opened the door. They rubbed Ike's head. Grandfather picked up Mem and said, "You are growing like a weed!"

"What does that mean?" Mem asked.

"It means you're growing fast," Grandfather said.

"Oh," Mem said. "Good!"

Later at the table Grandmother smiled and passed Ike more potatoes.

"Such a good appetite," she said to him.

"You'll grow up to be big and strong, like your father."

Ike didn't understand. His father was shorter than his mother. His father was weaker than his mother. His mother opened all the jars at home. Why couldn't he grow up to be like her?

Grandmother gave Ike a second piece of rhubarb pie. "I think the kids should stay with us awhile," she said, smiling.

Grandfather smiled and nodded.

Ike looked at his mother. She was smiling. Ike looked at his father. He was smiling. Ike looked at Mem. She was smiling. Everyone was smiling. Everyone, that is, except Ike. Ike was thinking about chores. Lots and lots of chores.

After supper everyone stepped out onto the front porch.

"Be good now and listen to Grandmother and Grandfather," Ike's father said to Ike.

Ike's mother bent down and looked into his eyes. "You'll have fun," she said. "You can ride the ponies." She kissed his cheek.

Ike's father picked up Mem and gave her a squeeze. He kissed her cheek.

"Grandmother and Grandfather will take good care of you," he said to her. "They even have a night-light in your room."

Mem sucked on her finger.

"You two just go on ahead," Grandmother said, taking Mem from her son. She smiled. "The kids always have a good time here."

Ike's parents climbed into the car. Ike's mother waved out the window.

"We'll see you on Sunday!" she called.

Ike and Mem and Grandmother and Grandfather waved back. The car drove away over the gravel. Its tires made crunching sounds. Then it was gone.

Suddenly Grandfather cupped his ear with his big hand. His eyes opened wide. "Do you hear that?" he whispered in a spooky voice. "*Listen!*"

All Ike heard was the cornfield rustling in the breeze. But he knew what Grandfather was doing. He'd done it to Ike when Ike was Mem's age.

"What is it?" Mem whispered. Her eyes opened very wide.

Grandfather leaned over and looked into her eyes.

"*Ghosts!*" he said. "They're saying '*Ooo-ooo! Ooo-ooo!*'" Then, very loudly, he said "*BOO!*" Mem jumped. Ike jumped too, even though he was expecting it.

"Manny!" Grandmother said sharply. "Stop scaring that child!" She set her hands on her hips.

Grandfather stood up straight. He put his hands in his pockets. "Sorry, Ev," he said.

"Well, we best do those dishes," Grandmother said. "They aren't going to do themselves."

Grandmother washed, Ike and Mem dried, and Grandfather put away. Then Ike and Mem went upstairs and got into their pajamas. They each kept pajamas, robes, and slippers at the farm. They brushed their teeth. They each kept toothbrushes at the farm too. They washed their faces and hands. Then they went to bed in different rooms.

Grandmother and Grandfather came up to tuck them in.

"Sleep tight," Grandmother said to each of them.

"Don't let the bedbugs bite," Grandfather said. Then he closed Ike's door behind him.

Night at the farm was very quiet. Ike could hear the cornfield outside. It was whispering in the wind. He could not hear what it was saying.

In the morning Grandmother came into Ike's room. The light from the hall shone in his eyes.

"Ike Nunn, are you still in bed?" she said.

Ike sat up in bed. He looked out the window. There were stars in the sky.

"Breakfast is ready," Grandmother said. She turned on the light. "And there are chores need doing."

Then she left. Ike heard her open Mem's door.

"Mem Nunn, are you still in bed?" she said.

"Chores," Ike muttered to himself. "Chores, chores, chores."

At home Ike only had to do a few chores. He had to make his bed, take out the garbage, help with the dishes, and mow the lawn.

But at the farm he always had lots of chores to do. Lots and lots of chores. Chores, chores, chores.

Ike made his bed and got dressed. Then he helped Mem make her bed and get dressed. They each kept spare clothes at the farm.

"It's dark out," Mem mumbled through her shirt.

"I know," Ike said as he pulled it down.

They brushed their teeth, washed their faces and hands, then went downstairs. Grandmother was in the kitchen, setting breakfast on the table.

"Eat up," she said. "You'll need your strength."

When Ike and Mem had finished eating, Grandmother gathered up their dishes.

"Best get on out to the yard," she said. "Your grandfather needs your help."

Ike and Mem pulled on their rubber boots. They each kept a pair of them at the farm. They went outside. The grass was damp with dew. The sun was peeking up over the corn-field.

Grandfather was in the yard pushing a wheelbarrow. The lawn was bigger than the baseball field at Ike's school.

"See all these acorns and sticks?" Grandfather asked, pointing at the lawn. There were lots of acorns and sticks lying in the grass.

"Yes sir," Ike said.

"I want you to pick them up for me," Grandfather said. He handed Ike a big bucket. "I need to mow tomorrow."

"Yes sir," Ike said.

"Then you best get on over to the garden," Grandfather said. "Your grandmother needs your help."

"Yes sir," Ike said.

Grandfather rolled the wheelbarrow into the toolshed. Then he walked to the machine shed, climbed on the tractor, and rode it out to the fields.

Ike and Mem picked up acorns and sticks. They picked up bucketfuls of acorns and sticks. Bucketfuls and bucketfuls of acorns and sticks. Then finally they were finished.

"We best get on over to the garden," Ike said, frowning.

"I know," Mem said. "Our grandmother needs our help."

The garden was bigger than the lawn.

Grandmother was there, digging with a little shovel. She wiped sweat from her brow with the back of her glove.

"Here you go," she said, handing Ike a big bucket. There were two pairs of gardening gloves inside. "Start over there." She pointed at the turnips.

"Yes ma'am," Ike said.

Ike and Mem pulled on their gloves and walked over to the turnips.

"I hate weeding," Mem said.

"I know," Ike said.

They pulled weeds from around the turnips. Then they pulled weeds from around the string beans, the onions, and the rutabagas.

"I hate rutabagas," Mem said.

"I know," Ike said.

They pulled weeds from around the peas, the carrots, the cabbages, and the beets.

"You hate beets," Ike said.

"I know," Mem said.

Then finally they were finished.

"We finished, Grandmother," Ike said.

Grandmother handed Ike another big bucket. It was full of dirty vegetables. She wiped her brow again with the back of her glove.

"Carry this up to the house for me," she said. "Then you best wash up for lunch."

"Yes ma'am," Ike said.

"Yes ma'am," Mem said too.

When Ike and Mem had finished lunch, Grandmother gathered up the dishes.

"Best get on out to the cornfield," she said. "Your grandfather needs your help."

Ike and Mem walked out to the cornfield. Grandfather was there holding a basket.

"Your grandmother needs corn," he said. "One basketful will do. Then bring it up to the porch and shuck it. I best get on over and feed the ponies." Then he walked away toward the barn.

"*I want to feed the ponies*," Mem said.

"I know," Ike said.

"I want to *ride* the ponies," Mem said.

"I know," Ike said. "But our grandmother needs corn."

They walked into the cornfield. It was bigger than the lawn and the garden and the baseball field at Ike's school all put together. The corn whispered in the wind.

"It's *ghosts*," Mem said softly. Her eyes opened wide.

"It's corn," Ike said. "Come on."

They walked and walked and walked. The row ahead went on forever.

"Why don't we pick the corn?" Mem asked.

Ike didn't answer. He was too upset to

answer. His friends were at home playing baseball. But he wasn't. He was doing chores. Lots and lots of chores. Chores, chores, chores.

They walked farther into the cornfield. Mem looked back. The row behind went on forever.

Finally Ike stopped walking. He set down the basket and sat down beside it. He put his face in his hands.

"What are you doing?" Mem asked. "Our grandmother needs corn!"

Ike just sat there. He just sat there in the dirt.

"No one can see us," he said at last. "No one can hear us."

Mem sat beside him. "No one?" she asked.

"No one," Ike said.

They sat quietly awhile, thinking. Then suddenly Ike said, "Chores, chores, chores!" He raised his voice. "GRANDMOTHER AND GRANDFATHER ARE THE WORST IN THE WORLD!"

Mem looked at him. He looked angry. "THE WORST IN THE WORLD!" she yelled too.

The two of them sat there in the dirt, feeling angry. Then Ike stood up.

"Come on," he said. "We best pick the corn."

Ike and Mem picked ear after ear of corn from the stalks and put them in the basket. When the basket was full, they walked back down the row. They walked and they walked and they walked.

Mem stopped. "Are we going the right way?" she asked.

"Just come on!" Ike said without stopping. "Keep up!"

Mem ran to catch up. They walked and they walked and they walked some more. The row ahead went on forever. Finally Ike could see the farmhouse through the corn.

"Come on, Mem!" he said. He started to run.

"Wait up!" Mem called after him.

At last they reached the edge of the corn-field. They saw the farmhouse and the garden and the barn and the old oak trees. They ran up to the house and ran up the porch steps. They sat on the porch swing and started shucking the corn. The silk stuck to every-thing.

Ike looked out at the cornfield. The corn was waving from side to side. It was whisper-ing in the wind. Ike stopped shucking. His eyes opened wide. He could hear what the corn was saying!

"Do you hear that?" he whispered to Mem.

"Hear what?" Mem whispered back.

Mem stopped shucking.

"The corn," Ike whispered. "It's whispering!"

Mem looked down at the ear of corn in her lap. She lifted it up to her ear.

"Not *that* corn!" Ike whispered. "*That* corn!" He pointed out to the cornfield.

Mem set down her ear of corn and listened to the cornfield. Her eyes opened wide. "It's *ghosts!*" she said.

"No!" Ike whispered. "It's the *corn*. It's saying something. Listen!"

They both sat very still and listened. The corn whispered in the wind.

"What's it saying?" Mem whispered.

Ike leaned over close to her. "It's saying,

'*Worst in the world! Worst in the world!*'" he whispered.

"Maybe they heard us," Mem whispered.

"Who heard us?" Ike whispered.

"The ears of corn," Mem whispered.

Ike looked at Mem. He looked at the ear of corn in her lap. He looked out at the cornfield. He looked back at Mem.

"What if Grandmother and Grandfather hear it?" he whispered.

Suddenly a voice called out, "Ike! Mem! Are you out there?"

It was Grandmother's voice from the kitchen. The window was right over their heads.

"Where's my corn?" she asked.

Ike's eyes opened very wide. Mem's opened even wider.

"We're almost done, Grandmother!" Ike said.

Ike and Mem started shucking as fast as they could. When they had finished, they carried the basket of corn inside.

"Get those muddy boots out of my clean kitchen!" Grandmother said to them.

Ike and Mem washed up, then they set the table.

Grandfather stepped into the kitchen in his stocking feet.

"Well, go on and get washed up," Grandmother said to him. "I'm putting the food on the table."

Ike and Mem helped her carry in the food. It smelled very good. Ike forgot all about the whispering of the corn. He ate two chicken legs and a thigh. He ate mashed potatoes with gravy, baked rutabagas, boiled beets, string beans, and buttered bread. He ate two ears of corn.

When they had finished eating, Grandmother took their plates into the kitchen. She came back with smaller plates and a rhubarb pie.

"Now," Grandmother said, smiling, "who'd like dessert?"

Everyone did.

Ike had two slices of rhubarb pie and four scoops of vanilla ice cream. The ice cream got melty. He liked it melty.

"Chores sure give a body an appetite," Grandmother said.

"They surely do," Grandfather said. He undid his belt.

Ike undid his too.

Then Grandmother said, "Just listen to that corn blowing in the wind."

Ike could hear the corn through the windows. It was saying, *Worst in the world! Worst in the world!*

"That's not the corn," Grandfather whispered in a spooky voice. His eyes opened wide. He leaned over close to Mem. "It's *ghosts!*" he said. "*Ooo-ooo! Ooo-ooo! BOO!*"

Mem jumped. So did Ike.

"Manny, I told you to stop scaring that child!" Grandmother said.

Grandfather sat back in his chair and put his hands in his lap. "Sorry, Ev," he said.

Grandmother stood up from the table. She set her hands on her hips. "Well, we best do those dishes," she said. "They aren't going to do themselves."

"Now you just let us take care of that," Grandfather said. "You go on into the other room and sit."

Grandmother sighed. She looked at Ike and Mem. They both smiled and nodded. "You know, I believe I will," she said.

Ike washed and Mem dried. Grandfather put away. Grandmother read a magazine in the living room in her chair.

"Manny," she called out once. "Did you know a cow had four stomachs?"

"I wish I had four stomachs," Grandfather said, patting his belly.

"So do I!" Ike laughed, patting his.

"Me too!" Mem said, patting hers.

After the dishes were done Grandfather said, "How about some cards?"

Ike and Mem nodded. They all went into the living room. Grandmother put down her magazine. The four of them played Crazy Eights. Ike won twice. Mem and Grandmother each won once. Grandfather did not win.

"Time for bed," he said.

Ike and Mem got into their pajamas. They brushed their teeth. They washed their faces and hands. Then they got into bed.

Grandmother and Grandfather came up to tuck them in. They tucked in Mem first. Then they tucked in Ike.

"Good night, Ike," Grandmother said. "Thanks for all the help today. There's always a lot to do around a farm."

"You're welcome," Ike said with a smile.

"Sleep tight," Grandmother said and turned out the light.

"Don't let the bedbugs bite," Grandfather said. He closed the door after them.

Ike felt very tired. His stomach felt very full. The bed was snug and warm. His room was dark and still. He heard the corn whispering outside. *"Worst in the world! Worst in the world!"*

Ike covered his head with his pillow. He wondered if Grandmother and Grandfather could hear the corn from downstairs in the living room.

An hour passed, then the light under Ike's door came on. Ike heard Grandmother and Grandfather walk down the hall to their bedroom. Then the light under his door went out. His room was dark again.

"Worst in the world! Worst in the world!" the corn whispered outside.

Ike wondered if Grandmother and Grandfather could hear it in their bedroom.

Then Ike heard his door open a crack.

"Ike?" a voice whispered. "You awake?" It was Mem. She ran into the room and jumped up on Ike's bed. She was wearing her robe and slippers.

"The ghosts are keeping me awake," she whispered.

"It's not ghosts," Ike said, sitting up. "It's the corn."

Ike looked out the window. There were stars in the sky. He looked out over the dark cornfield. The corn was waving in the wind. He thought for a second, then he whispered, "Come on!"

He slipped out of bed and slipped on his

robe. He stepped into his slippers and tiptoed out into the hall. Mem followed. They tiptoed downstairs, through the dining room, and into the kitchen. Ike opened a drawer. He took out a flashlight and turned it on. Then he and Mem tiptoed outside. They pulled on their rubber boots. They tiptoed down the porch steps. Then they ran across the yard toward the cornfield.

Ike stood at the edge and listened.

"*Worst in the world! Worst in the world!*" the corn said.

"Come on!" Ike said.

He ran into the cornfield. Mem followed. The row went on forever. They ran and they ran and they ran. They ran until they couldn't run anymore. Then they sat down on the

ground. They were tired. They were cold. They huddled together in the dirt. Ike closed his eyes and took a deep breath.

"OUR GRANDPARENTS ARE *NOT* THE WORST IN THE WORLD!" he said in a loud voice.

He hoped the ears of corn could hear him.

Mem looked up at Ike. He looked worried. "*NOT* THE WORST IN THE WORLD!" she yelled too.

Then Ike stood up. "Come on," he said.

Ike ran down the row. Mem followed. They ran and they ran and they ran. The row went on forever. They ran and they ran and they ran some more.

"Are we going the right way?" Mem asked, huffing and puffing.

"Just keep up!" Ike called back to her.

They ran and they ran and they ran even more. They could not see the farmhouse through the corn. They could not see the barn or the oak trees. They could see only the corn and the stars in the sky.

"I can't run anymore!" Mem said. She stopped running and began to cry.

Ike stopped running too. He took her hand.

"We'll walk," he said. "I think we're almost there."

They walked and they walked and they walked. They walked some more. Then Ike stopped. His eyes opened wide.

"Do you hear that?" he whispered.

"Hear what?" Mem whispered back. She wiped tears from her cheeks with her sleeve.

"The corn!" Ike whispered. "It's whispering!"

Mem listened. Her eyes opened wide. "It's *ghosts!*" she whispered.

"No!" Ike said. "It's the corn! It's saying something! Listen!"

They both sat very still and listened.

"I hear it!" Mem whispered. "It's saying, 'Ike! Mem! Ike! Mem!'"

Ike looked at her. He smiled. "It's not the corn!" he said. "It's Grandmother and Grandfather!"

Ike ran toward the sound of his grandparents' voices. Mem ran after him.

Finally Ike could see the farmhouse through the corn. All the lights were on. He saw Grandmother and Grandfather. They were standing at the edge of the cornfield. They were wearing their robes and slippers.

"Grandfather!" Mem squealed. She ran past Ike and jumped into Grandfather's arms.

Grandfather smiled. "You *are* growing like a weed!" he said.

Grandmother held Ike's head in her hands. She looked straight into his eyes. "Just what

were you doing out here in the middle of the night?" she said. Then she wiped a tear from her cheek with her sleeve.

"We had to talk to the corn," Mem said.

"It was scaring Mem," Ike said. "We came out to tell it to be quiet."

Grandfather laughed. Grandmother did not.

"I told you to stop scaring that child!" she said with a scowl.

Grandfather looked down at his slippers. "Sorry, Ev," he said.

Grandmother set her hands on her hips. "Well, we'll catch our death of cold out here," she said. "Let's get inside."

She started toward the house. Ike and Grandfather followed. Grandfather carried Mem.

Grandmother and Grandfather tucked Mem into bed. Ike heard Grandfather tell her that there were positively no ghosts. Then they tucked in Ike.

"How did you know we were out there?" Ike asked Grandmother.

"The corn blowing in the wind woke me up," she said. "But then I listened harder, and it wasn't the corn at all. It was you two."

"Oh," Ike said. He looked at Grandmother's face. Her eyes looked tired and red. "I'm sorry," he said.

"Just sleep good and tight," Grandmother said. She tucked his covers under his mattress. Then she turned out the light and stepped out into the hall.

"There aren't any ghosts," Grandfather whispered to Ike. "I was just kidding around. There aren't any bedbugs either."

Ike smiled. "I know," he said.

The next day was Sunday.

After breakfast Ike and Mem helped Grandmother feed the animals. They fed the cows, the chickens, and the ponies.

"One day I'll get a pony," Mem said.

"Where will you keep it?" Ike asked.

"I'll get a farm to go with it," Mem said.

Grandfather mowed the lawn with the riding lawn mower. Ike and Mem took turns riding with him. The lawn mower was very noisy. Ike loved it.

"GO FASTER, GRANDFATHER!" he yelled.

"WHAT?" Grandfather yelled back.

Then Grandmother and Grandfather saddled the ponies. Ike rode Thistle. Grandmother rode Paint. Mem rode Candy Apple with Grandfather. They rode around the lawn and the garden. They rode all the way around the cornfield. The corn whispered in the breeze.

Ike couldn't hear what it was saying.

"The corn sure sounds pretty," Grandmother said. She looked at Grandfather.

Grandfather smiled and nodded. Ike and Mem smiled and nodded too.

After lunch Ike heard tires crunching on the gravel. It was the car.

Ike's mother hugged Ike and Mem. She picked up Mem in her arms.

"Did you miss us?" she asked Mem. "Did you have fun?"

"We did a lot of chores," Mem said.

Grandmother laughed. "They were a big help," she said.

Grandfather nodded.

"We rode the lawn mower!" Ike said. "And the ponies!"

"I rode Candy Apple," Mem said. "She's the best one."

Ike liked Thistle the best.

"Grandmother and Grandfather are *not* the worst in the world!" Mem said.

Ike's mother laughed. Ike's father laughed. Grandmother and Grandfather laughed. Mem laughed. And this time, Ike laughed too.